McBlack

www.jasonfranks.com
www.blackglasspress.com

Copyright © Jason Franks 2010-2017
Edited by Jason Franks
Cover Art: Ron Salas
Cover Art Chapter 1: Jason Franks
Cover Art Chapter 2: Rhys McDonald
Cover Art Chapter 3: Tom Bonin

MCBLACK VOLUME 1. October 2017. 3rd Edition.

Printed in Australia.

ISBN: 978-0-9805167-4-6

McBLACK

SCRIPT / PENCILS / LETTERING:
JASON FRANKS

INKS / FINISHES:
DAVE GUTIERREZ

www.jasonfranks.com
www.blackglasspress.com

1: THE GENTLE ART OF MAKING ENEMIES

THEY USED TO SAY 'THE CITY IS A CHARACTER.'
THEY USED TO SAY ALL KINDS OF THINGS, BUT THAT WAS BEFORE THE B&W SOCIETY HIRED ME TO BURN DOWN THE WRITER'S GUILD.

HESE DAYS THERE'S A LOT LESS EOPLE TALKING, WHICH I GUESS WHY YOU'RE LISTENING TO THE KES OF ME.

MY NAME IS WHITEFACE MCBLACK, AND I DO BAD THINGS FOR MONEY.
TAX ACCOUNTANT
TAXIDERMIST

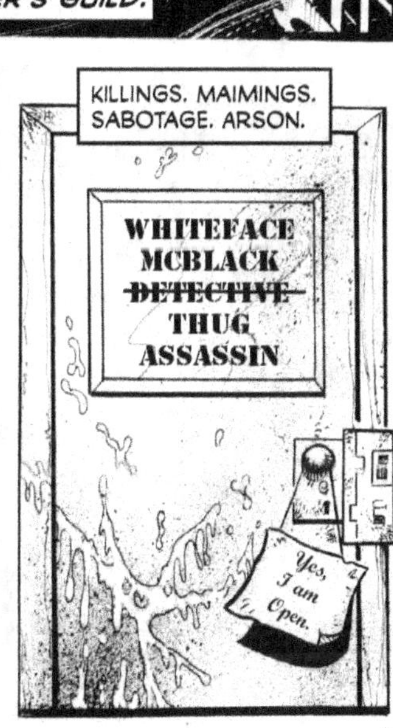

KILLINGS. MAIMINGS. SABOTAGE. ARSON.
WHITEFACE MCBLACK
DETECTIVE
THUG
ASSASSIN
Yes, I am Open.

WHITEFACE
MCBLACK
A
COME ON IN.
I GUESS THAT MAKES ME A BAD PERSON, BUT, HONESTLY?

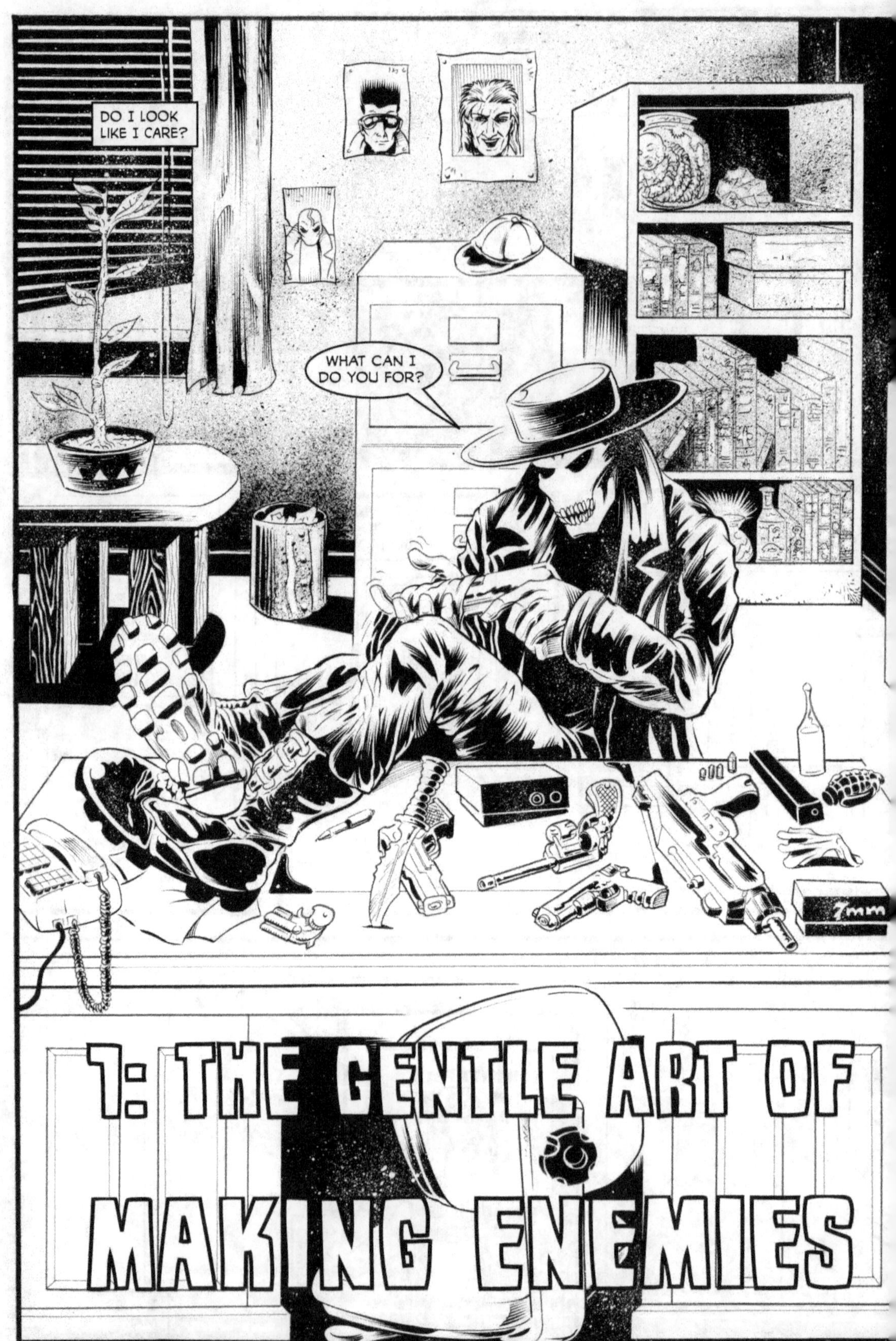

DO I LOOK LIKE I CARE?
WHAT CAN I DO YOU FOR?
7mm
1: THE GENTLE ART OF MAKING ENEMIES

OP ME IF YOU'VE ARD THIS ONE ORE:
MR MCBLACK, I NEED YOU TO FIND MY EX-HUSBAND.
SORRY, LADY. I DON'T DO THAT KINDA WORK ANY MORE.
HE TOOK EVERYTHING I HAD. MY FORTUNE, MY HOUSE, MY TITLES... EVERY-THING...
"IT ALL BEGAN WHEN THE KILLER DAME WALKED INTO MY OFFICE."
YEAH, I'VE HEARD IT, TOO--WITH WEARYING MONOTONY.
REAL SORRY TO HEAR THAT.
WHY DON'T YOU TRY LENNY TWO-EYES, UP THE STREET? HE'S A LAWYER; HE'LL GET YOUR STUFF BACK.
MR. MCBLACK, I DON'T CARE ABOUT GETTING MY 'STUFF' BACK...
WHAT I WANT IS REVENGE.
WHAT DID YOU SAY HIS NAME WAS?

THE DAME TOLD ME THAT DUKE DAVID OBERG--HER ROTTEN EX-- HAD TAKEN HER TITLES AND ESTATE, SO THAT WAS THE FIRST PLACE I DECIDED TO LOOK.

TURNED OUT, IT WASN'T EXACTLY DIFFICULT TO FIND.
Chateau Oberg
YEAH, WHAT DO YOU WANT?

I'M LOOKIN' FOR YOUNG DAVID OBERG.
WHO IS THIS?

HIS AUNTIE ETHEL.

I KNEW THE DAME WAS LYING TO ME.

YOU DON'T HIRE A LOW-RENT THUG LIKE ME TO FIND A MISSING NOB, NO MATTER HOW BIG AN ARSEHOLE HE IS.
I MAKE TOO MUCH MESS.
PRIDE MYSELF ON IT, IN FACT.
IT WASN'T MAKING A LICK OF SENSE, BUT SUDDENLY THE CASE WAS LOOKING A WHOLE LOT MORE INTERESTING THAN I HAD FIRST THOUGHT.

I SMELL BACON.
WELL, I WOULD, IF I HAD A NOSE... BUT YOU GET THE PICTURE:
COPS. THE BEST-ARMED AND MOST BRUTAL CRIMINAL SYNDICATE IN THE CITY.
COME WITH US, AUNTIE ETHEL. THE LIEUTENANT WANTS TO SEE YOU
SING IT WITH ME, BOYS...
LIKE I SAID: THIS WAS ACTUALLY STARTING TO GET INTERESTING.
"...WHAT'S THE COLOUR OF A 2C PIECE...?"

WELL, WELL. LOOK WHO'S ON THE JOB.

MCBLACK!
GLORING AND I GO BACK A WAYS.

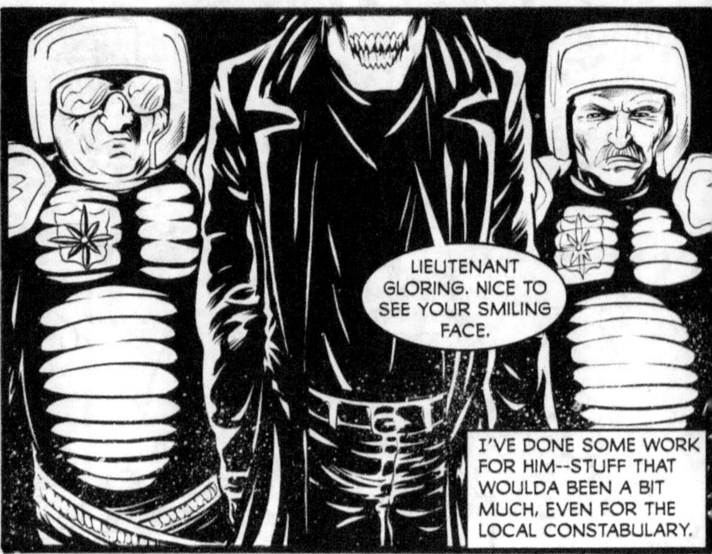

LIEUTENANT GLORING. NICE TO SEE YOUR SMILING FACE.
I'VE DONE SOME WORK FOR HIM--STUFF THAT WOULDA BEEN A BIT MUCH, EVEN FOR THE LOCAL CONSTABULARY.

DON'T LIKE HIM ANY MORE'N HE LIKES ME, BUT HIS MONEY'S AS GOOD AS ANYBODY ELSE'S.
YOU'RE LOOKING FOR DAVE OBERG, HUH?
I TAKE IT HE AIN'T HERE?

ABDUCTED, WE THINK.. BUT THERE'S NO RANSOM NOTE.

ANY SUSPECTS?
NOT YET.
YOU SPOKEN TO HIS EX-WIFE?

HE HAS AN EX?

I SEE YOU GOT THE MATTER WELL IN HAND.

GLORING'S BODYGUARD AND CHIEF ENFORCER, SERGEANT JAYNA. EX-GREEN BERET.
KIDNAPPING, JESUS... I CAN'T BE WASTING MY TIME ON THIS CRAP.
I HAVE A BUSINESS TO RUN.

WELL, WHY DON'T YOU JUST CLOSE THE BOOKS ON THIS ONE?
I'M GETTING PAID TO SETTLE THE MATTER.

HEY, SO LONG AS SOMEBODY GETS SOMETHING OUT OF IT.
DOESN'T SAY MUCH, BUT SHE IS SOMEBODY NOT TO BE FUCKED WITH.

MUCH AS I ADMIRE OUR POLICE FORCE FOR THEIR DEDICATION AND THEIR ALMOST-UNLIMITED ACCESS TO HEAVY MUNITIONS, THE UNFORTUNATE TRUTH IS THAT THEY JUST AREN'T VERY BRIGHT.
SEE THAT FLAG? THE PIG-DOG WITH THE TUSKS?
THAT ISN'T ANY KIND OF NOB CREST.
THOSE ARE THE COLOURS OF A BIKER GANG CALLED THE THRUPENNY BOARDOGS.
THING IS, THOSE CUSTOM BIKES THAT THE BOARDOGS LIKE TO RIDE ARE EXPENSIVE.
BEING A MOTORCYCLE HOODLUM IS NO LONGER A LOW-RENT GIG, LIKE, SAY... BEING A PRIVATE DICK.
MOST OF THESE BIKERS ARE PROFESSIONALS DURING THE WEEK.
DOCTORS, LAWYERS, STOCK BROKERS...

SO IT'S ONLY LOGICAL THAT THE BOARDOGS WOULD HAVE A CORPORATE HQ.
THINGS HAVE CHANGED A LITTLE SINCE THEIR VAGABOND DAYS.
SO MAYBE THEY'RE A BIT SOFTER THAN THEY USED TO BE.
BETTER FED, BETTER FINANCED, BETTER ORGANIZED.
BETTER ARMED.
BUT THE REAL REASON THE BOARDOGS ARE STILL DANGEROUS...

...IS THAT THEY'RE ALL MUTANTS AND CYBORGS.
--LUBBER'S ON SITTING THERE ON THIS GARBAGE-WAGON...
...IT'S FUCKING SHOWROOM CHERRY. HAS THAT SPORTSTER ENGINE IN IT, BARELY 1000CC...
OR, SOMETIMES, THEY'RE BOTH.
YEP, THAT'S RIGHT.
HELLO? CAN I HELP YOU?
CORPORATE MUTANT CYBORG BIKERS.
HI, YES. I'M HERE TO INQUIRE ABOUT THE ABDUCTION OF BIG DAVE OBERG?

COULDN'T MAKE THIS SHIT UP IF I TRIED.

SO, WHO DO I SPEAK TO ABOUT OBERG, AGAIN?
UM...

OH, NEVER MIND.

WHO'S IN CHARGE HERE?

OOPS.
DON'T WORRY, IT'S A BLOOD BAG.
SERIOUSLY.
BOOM!

I AM.

RRRRRRRRRRRRRRRRRRRRRRRRRRRRRRRRRR

WELL, THAT WAS QUITE EXCITING.
OKAY. SO. WHERE IS DAVID OBERG?
IF YOU DON'T MIND MY ASKING?
WLUDARSKI HAS HIM AT THE ASHRAM.
WHAT DOES HE WANT OBERG FOR?
HE THINKS OBERG HAS THE DELUCCI BAMBINO.
BUT YOU'RE WASTING YOUR TIME. IF HE EVER DID HAVE IT, HE'S LOST IT NOW.
AH, SEE, WELL... HERE'S THE THING:
I DON'T GIVE A FUCK ABOUT THE DELUCCI BAMBINO.

AFTER A QUICK STOP AT THE OFFICE A CHANGE OF CLOTHES I NIPPED OVER TO THE BOARDOGS' ASHRAM.
'ASHRAM', THEY CALL IT, BUT IT'S AN OLD ARMY BUNKER, LEFT OVER FROM THE DE-NATIONALIZATION WARS.
ABOUT WHAT YOU'D EXPECT FROM A BUNCH OF CORPORATE MUTANT CYBORG BIKER HIPPIES, I GUESS.

SEEMED THE BAMBINO WASN'T THE BOARDOGS' MOST IMMEDIATE PROBLEM, THOUGH.
THESE GUYS IN THE NOVELTY VEHICLES ARE THE SCREAMING MICKS--A STREET GANG AFFILIATED THE EMERALD ISLE REPUBLICAN ARMY.

IRISH PARAMILITARY CANNIBALS, OBVIOUSLY.

I THINK I'M GONNA ENJOY THIS PART.

IT'S ALL HAPPENING HERE TONIGHT AT THE ASHRAM, FOLKS!
IN THE GREEN:
TABITHA O'CONNELL; SCREAMING MICKS' OPS COMMANDER AND UNDOUBTED BADASS.
THAT'S IT, ME BOYOS--
--EVERY LAST FOOKIN' ONE OF TEM!
NO PRISONERS!!
IN PAISLEY AND BLACK; IN PASTELS AND CHAINS:
REG WLUDARSKY; EX-CON, GURU AND SPIRITUAL CHAIRMAN OF THE BOARDOGS.
FOR KRISHNAH! FOR KALI! FOR JOHN PAUL XXX!
DING DING! MAY THE BEST FREAK ARMY WIN!

TIME TO PICK A SIDE.

IF THE MICKS WIN, I'LL NEVER FIND OUT WHAT THE BOARDOGS DID WITH OBERG.
PROBLEM IS, THE DOGS ARE LOSING.

AH, WHAT THE HELL. MY FRIEND LILA GIVES ME A BULK PRICES ON AMMO--
MAY AS WELL ENJOY IT.

T'EY'RE CHEWIN' US TE BITS!

RETREAT, BEGORRAH!
MAYBE IT'S JUST THE ACCENT, BUT... I ADMIT IT. I'M TURNED ON.

...THE POLITE THING WOULD BE TO SAY *THANK YOU*.

...WHO THE HELL ARE *YOU*?

I'M THE ONE WHO SHOT UP YOUR CORPORATE HQ THIS MORNING.

BUT NOW YOU'RE ON OUR SIDE?

NOPE.

I'M JUST HERE FOR DAVID OBERG.
OBERG NEVER ARRIVED HERE.

THE MICKS CAME INSTEAD.

OH.

WASN'T TIL AFTER I LEFT THAT I THOUGHT TO ASK WHAT THE E.I.R.A.'S PROBLEM WITH THE BOARDOGS WAS.
I GUESS THAT WAS A MISTAKE, BUT I WAS STARTING TO GET BORED OF THE BOARDOGS...
... AND I WANTED TO SAY GOODBYE BEFORE THE FRIENDSHIP GOT STALE.
OH, WELL. FUN WHILE IT LASTED.

THE SCREAMING MICKS LIVE OFF THE COAST ON THE EMERALD ISLE, WHICH THEY LIKE TO THINK OF AS THEIR OWN SOVEREIGN STATE.

CHIEF CROPS ARE POTATOES AND COCONUTS. THEY EXPORT STOUT, WHISKEY, NATIVE HANDICRAFTS, AND AUTOMATIC GUNFIRE.

MOSTLY, THEY TRADE FOR AMMUNITION AND HUMAN FLESH.
DESPITE THE NATURAL BEAUTY OF THE ISLAND AND THE QUAINT TRADITIONS OF THE NATIVES, THE TOURIST INDUSTRY JUST AIN'T WHAT IT COULD BE.

SOME CALL IT A BREEDING GROUND FOR TERROR.

I LIKE TO THINK OF IT AS A LOST PARADISE.

G'DAY, FELLAS!
I'VE BEEN LOOKING FOR DAVID OBERG AND I WONDER IF YOU FINE
LADS AND LASSIES MIGHT HAPPEN TO HAVE HIM HERE??

I DON'T THINK SO, MON.
WE'RE NOT MUCH GOOD WIT' DE P.O.W.S.
NOT MUCH GOOD AT ALL.

DON'T SPARE TE LEAD, ME BOYOS--
THERE ISN'T MUCH MEAT TO BE HAD ON HIM, ANYWAY.

WELL, OKAY, THEN.

AH, SHIT.
I HATE IT WHEN I LOSE.
SHIT.
LEAVE HIM FOR DE BUZZARDS, BEJAYSUS-MON.
DINNER'S GETTING COLD.

DON'T GET
ME WRONG--

--I DON'T ENJOY BEING
SHOT, STABBED, BEATEN,
UP AND IMPALED ANY
BETTER THAN YOU
WOULD.

BUT, SOMETIMES?

SOMETIMES?

HEY,
FELLAS?
I HATE TO
INTERRUPT
YOU AT DINNER
TIME, AND ALL,
BUT...

IS THERE ANY
CHANCE YOU'VE
REMEMBERED
WHAT YOU DID TO
DAVE OBERG
YET?
SOMETIMES,
IT'S WORTH IT.

WHERE'S OBERG?
THE BOARDOGS WERE SUPPOSED TO HAVE HIM AT THE ASHRAM.

HE WAS NEVER THERE.
AND HOW WERE WE TE KNOW?
ANY IDEA WHERE HE MIGHT HAVE GONE?
NONE.

YOU AFTER THE BAMBINO, TOO?
THE WHAT?

THE DELUCCI BAMBINO?

...UH, NO.

TE BASTARD SCREWED US ON A WEAPONS DEAL, DON'T YE KNOW?

OBERG WAS DEALING WEAPONS?

HE'S JUST A BROKER.
WHO'S HIS SUPPLIER?
DON'T KNOW. SOMEBODY GOVERNMENT.

HUH.

WELL, THANKS FOR HAVING ME.

IT'S BEEN A REAL PLEASURE.

SORRY ABOUT YOUR SPEAR.

SKINNY WHITE BITCH.

SO, MY QUARRY WAS A TITLE-STEALING, WIFE-DESERTING, ANTIQUITY-HUNTING ARMS DEALER?
THE MORE CLUES I FOUND, THE LESS SENSE IT ALL MADE.
THE DAME WAS LYING; I'D KNOWN THAT SINCE PAGE 4.
MAYBE EVERYONE WAS LYING.
BUT I DIDN'T CARE. I WAS STARTING TO ENJOY MYSELF.
THREE SETS OF CLOTHES, FIVE LIARS, SIXTY-ODD BODIES AND 400 ROUNDS IN VARIOUS CALIBERS--
--IT MAY NOT SOUND LIKE MUCH, BUT I WAS JUST STARTING TO GET WARMED UP.
TO BE CONTINUED, 'EY?

2: KILL THE BODY AND THE HEAD WILL DIE

BRIGHT AND EARLY THE NEXT DAY I WENT TO FIND LILA BODICKER.
LILA'S THE BIGGEST WEAPONS DEALER IN THE CITY.
TOUGH MARKET, BUT HER COMPETITORS JUST DON'T SEEM TO LAST VERY LONG.
I DECIDED IT WOULD BE BEST TO APPROACH HER AWAY FROM HER OFFICE.
MCBLACK! FANCY SEEIN' YOU HERE.
YOU KNOW--TRY BEING A BIT MORE DISCRETE.
GOTTA WALK MY DOG SOMEWHERE.
NEVER FIGURED YOU FOR A DOG FANCIER.
CROWD I'VE BEEN HANGING WITH LATELY?
YOU'D BE SURPRISED.
SO I BROUGHT WHITEFACE MCDOG WITH ME.
SHUT UP. SHE'S MEANER THAN SHE LOOKS.

HANGING, AS IN, YOU ACTUALLY HAVE FRIENDS?
OR HANGING FROM THE END OF A ROPE?
KIND OF FRIENDS I HAVE, THERE AIN'T MUCH DIFFERENCE.
WORD IS, THE E.I.R.A. GOT STIFFED ON AN ARMS DEAL BROKERED BY DAVID OBERG.

THE OBERG WHO'S BEEN IN ALL THE TABLOIDS?
LORD OBERG?
THE VERY ONE.
YOU KNOW HIM?
NOT YET, I DON'T.

YOU KNOW OF ANY MILITARY SOURCES WHO MIGHT BE DEALING BEHIND YOUR BACK?

MILITARY? NO WAY.

THE ONLY ONES THAT STUPID WOULD BE THE--
LILA.

I SEE EM.

THE WEST END REAPERS.
RUNNER'S UP IN THIS YEAR'S DIVISION 3 METRO MIXED FOOTBALL LEAGUE.
THEY RAISE A LOT OF FUNDS THROUGH FREELANCE ASSASSINATIONS.
GUNSHY--
LOCK AND LOAD.
WHURF WHURF WHURF!
ARF ARF ARF!
HACK... HYACK...
KKCHICKETY
AR-HOO?
HYEH.
KKRCHAK

GOOD DOGGY.
GOOD DOG.
...HENH HENH HENH...

IS THAT IT?

I GUESS SO.

YOU GOT SOMETHING ON YOU.
OH. THANKS.
WHAT WAS THAT ALL ABOUT, ANYWAY?

HELL IF I KNOW.
HERE, LET ME HELP YOU WITH THAT.

YOU WERE SAYIN'...
...BEFORE WE WERE SO RUDELY INTERRUPTED...

I WAS SAYING, THE ONLY PEOPLE STUPID ENOUGH
TO DEAL ARMS BEHIND MY BACK WOULD BE THE--
WHOA.

SOCCER PLAYERS.
I SHOULDA KNOWN SHE WAS FAKING.

AW, SHIT.

C'MON, DOGFACE.

AND THAT WAS WHEN I KNEW HOW IT WAS ALL GOING TO END.
WE'RE DONE HERE.

I WAS PRETTY SURE I'D WORKED OUT WHO STUPID ENOUGH TO WHOLESALE ARMS BEHIND LILA'S BACK, BUT I DIDN'T KNOW WHAT THEY HAD TO DO WITH OBERG.
I DECIDED TO GO BACK TO THE DAME, ASK HER SOME QUESTIONS.
HMMM.

DIDN'T EXPECT MUCH TRUTH OUT OF HER, BUT SOMETIMES LIES ARE JUST AS USEFUL.

WHAT DO YOU WANT?
I'M LOOKING FOR, UM... THE KILLER DAME?
SHE HAVE A NAME?

NOPE.

HUH.

I GUESS SHE DOES HAVE ONE--EVEN IF IT BELONGS TO SOMEONE ELSE.
scott unde
kaila weinst
reginald st jo
darryl trotma
huckleberry ho
ame Oberg
mlle. from armen

IT'S MCBLACK.
WHERE ARE YOU?
THE LOBBY OF YOUR MOTEL.
WHAT ROOM ARE YOU IN?
UH, I'LL MEET YOU ON THE ROOF.

I'LL BE RIGHT UP.

MCBLACK, HOW'S THE CASE GOING?
INTERESTING, TO SAY THE LEAST.
YOUR EX IS INVOLVED WITH A WHOLE LOTTA BAD PEOPLE.
LOT OF BAD PEOPLE IN THIS TOWN, MCBLACK.
THAT'S WHY I HIRED YOU.
I'M JUST MISUNDERSTOOD.
MISUNDERSTOOD LIKE A BULLET IN THE HEAD.
UH...
HOLD THAT THOUGHT. THERE'S SOMETHING I GOTTA GO DEAL WITH.

GUNS 'N' TOYS
THIS GUY.

I'VE TANGLED WITH HIM BEFORE.

I'LL BE BACK IN A MINUTE.
HE BEAT THE LIVING FUCK OUT OF ME.
NOT LIKE WHAT THE MICKS DID. I MEAN, THIS GUY REALLY TOOK ME APART.

THIS GUY'S SPECIAL.

BUT THEN, SO AM I.
WHY ELSE WOULD I BE COMING BACK FOR MORE?

SEE WHERE THE SHOTGUN CAME FROM? NOPE?
ME NEITHER. TOLD YOU HE WAS SPECIAL.

UNLIMITED WEAPONS, PLUS HE'S FASTER, STRONGER, AND TOUGHER THAN 'MOST EVERYONE.

BULLET PROOF, TOO.
A BAD MOTHERFUCKER NO DOUBT ABOUT IT.

I GOT A BIGGER VOCABULARY THAN HE DOES, THOUGH.

LOOK AT HIM, EMPTY HANDS...

AND HE'S STILL FASTER ON THE DRAW.

OH, YOU GOTTA
BE KIDDING ME.

OWIE OWIE OWIE.

OUCH.

GODDAMN.

DIDN'T THINK THAT WOULD WORK.

HE'S STRONG AS AN OX AND I'M AS WEAK AS SINGLE-PLY TOILET PAPER.
I GUESS THAT'S ONE DRAWBACK OF NOT HAVING AN ACTUAL BOD

NOW THIS IS JUST GODDAMN EMBARRASSING.

...I DON'T THINK I LIKE WHERE THIS IS GOING.
HEY. HEY!
HEY!
TODAY STARTED WITH AN IMPALEMENT AND ENDED WITH A BEHEADING...
BUT FROM HERE ON OUT, THINGS ARE DEFINITELY LOOKING UP.
ASSHOLE.

SO, UH...
WHAT WAS ALL THAT ABOUT?
I WAS HIRED TO KILL THAT GUY A WHILE BACK.
DIDN'T QUITE WORK OUT.
THAT WAS YOUR SECOND ATTEMPT?

I'VE LOST COUNT.

YOU DON'T SEEM PARTICULARLY EMBARASSED.
ACTUALLY, I'M GLAD YOU WERE THERE.

REALLY?
OF COURSE.
YOU HAVE ANY IDEA HOW DIFFICULT IT IS TO ROLL UP THESE STAIRS?

SMELLS LIKE DOGSHIT IN HERE.
I MUST'VE STEPPED IN SOMETHING.

IN THERE.

KILLER WARDROBE YOU GOT THERE.
JUST PUT ME DOWN ON THE FLOOR AND CLOSE THE DOOR.

NO PEEKING. I'M SHY.
SHY? YOU DON'T EVEN HAVE A BODY.

WELL, THAT'S EVER STOPPED ME LOOKIN' GOOD.
NOT BAD, FOR A GUY WHO'S JUST A HEAD.
WHO SAYS YOU GOTTA HAVE SKIN TO BE SEXY?
SO, TELL ME--
DID YOU KNOW YOUR EX- WAS DEALING ARMS TO THE E.I.R.A.?
THAT WAS A ONE TIME THING.
HE NEEDED MONEY FOR ONE OF HIS STUPID SCHEMES.
YOU HAVE ANY IDEA WHO HIS SUPPLIER WAS?
NOPE... BUT HIS OLD PARTNER MIGHT.
THIS PARTNER HAVE A NAME?

ZMILING
ZIEGFRIED'S
ZALE
TURNS OUT, THE PARTNER WAS PRETTY EASY TO FIND.
RIGHT THERE IN THE YELLOW PAGES: ZMILING ZIEGFRIED, FORMER WRESTLER TURNED MONSTER TRUCK DEALER.
MAY I ASSIST YOU IN FULFILLING YOUR AUTOMOBILE-CRUSHING DREAMS?
AFTERNOON, SIR.
NOPE.
IS ZERE A PROBLEM HERE?
NOPE.
PERHAPS I CAN HELP YOU MIT SOMEZING?
PERHAPS.
I'M LOOKING FOR YOUR OLD PARTNER, DAVE OBERG.
LET'S GO TO MY OFFICE.

WOW. I'M GLAD HE'S GIVEN UP THE PINK SPANDEX.
I HAF NOT ZEEN DAFID IN VEEKS.
I'M NOT SURPRISED.
BESIDES ME, HE HAS TWO GANGS, A TERRORIST ORGANIZATION, THE COPS, AND AN ANGRY EX-WIFE OUT LOOKING FOR HIM.

I TOLD HIM HE VAS BITINK OFF MORE ZAN HE COULD CHEW.

DO TELL?

DEALING MIT ZOSE SCHWEIN, UNT GOINK TO ZOSE OZZER SCHWEINHUNDTS...
I TOLD HIM HE VAS KRAZY.
SCHWEIN AND SCHWEINHUNDTS?
I HAF ALREADY TOLD YOU FAR TOO MUCH.

ACTUALLY, YOU'VE TOLD ME PLENTY.

TRY NOT TO GET YOUR HEAD ZSTUCK IN ZE DOOR.

NO NEW INFORMATION, BUT OL' ZIGGY'S PDIGIN ENGLISH HAD JUST CONFIRMED WHAT I SUSPECTED.
HUH?
THURLOW LEE AND HIS REDNECK TRIADS.
I SHOULD HAVE EXPECTED SOMETHING THIS, SHOULDN'T I?
OH, MAN.
ZER BATTLE... IS JOINED!
ZIGGY, COULD YOU AT LEAST PUT ON SOME PANTS?
JUST WHAT I NEEDED--
THE FAT GUY IN A PINK LEOTARD ON MY TEAM.

I WANT
AVE OBERG,
BOY!
I WANT YOUR
SCUMBAG PARTNER
OR I WANT THE CODE
FOR THE DRUGS!
CODE?
DRUGS?
IT'S
A LONG
ZTORY.
AREN'T
THEY ALL?

THE FAT MAN GOES DOWN.
THEY WON'T KILL ZIGGY, THEY STILL NEED INFORMATION FROM HIM.
COURSE, SO DO I.
WHAT I DON'T NEED ARE THESE TRIADS.

I LOVE MONSTER TRUCKS.
NOT BECAUSE THEY'RE HUGE AND INDESTRUCTIBLE...
NOT BECAUSE THEY'RE A GOOD WAY TO GET FROM 'A' TO 'B'...
NO, I LOVE MONSTER TRUCKS...

...BECAUSE THEY HAVE SUCH BIG FUEL TANKS.
BOOM.
2: KILL THE BODY AND THE HEAD WILL DIE

OK, I ADMIT IT.
THAT HURT LIKE FUCK.
BUT HELL IF THE RUSH WASN'T WORTH IT.
ZIGGY'S USELESS IN A FIGHT, BUT HE SEEMS TO HAVE RUNNING AWAY DOWN PAT.
THAT'S OKAY. I CAN FIND HIM AGAIN WHEN IF I NEED HIM.

SO, THURLOW. YOU KNOW WHO I AM?

AH DON'T KNOW NOTHIN', MCBLACK.

TELL ME ABOUT THE DRUGS, THURLOW.
AH CAIN'T...

THURLOW.
I... HE ARRANGED A SHIPMENT FOR US.
TOOK HALF THE CASH UP FRONT AND GAVE US HALF A CODE FOR THE LOCATION.

THEN HE DISAPPEARED.
THAT'S IT. THAT'S THE WHOLE STORY.

THAT'S CAUSE HE'S BEEN KIDNAPPED ABOUT EIGHT TIMES SINCE TUESDAY.
STICK AROUND, THURLOW; THIS AIN'T OVER YET.
TO BE CONCLUDED!
(WELL, KIND OF.)

3: ON THE RICOCHET

THREE DAYS IN, AND I WAS SICK OF FOLLOWING THE TRAIL, PICKING UP CLUES.
SO I CAME UP WITH A PLAN.
MAYBE NOT THE MOST ELEGANT OF PLANS, BUT ONE I WAS PRETTY SURE WOULD PUT THE CASE DOWN ONCE AND FOR ALL.

ALL THAT WAS LEFT WAS TO CHOOSE THE BEST WEAPON FOR THE JOB.

HI, IT'S McBLACK.
MEET ME AT THE OFFICE.
WE'RE GONNA GO FINISH THIS.

COME PREPARED-- IT'S GONNA BE UGLY.

I MADE A FEW MORE CALLS WHILE I WAITED FOR THE DAME; GETTING EVERYONE IN THE RIGHT PLACE.
I THOUGHT I SAID TO COME PREPARED?
BACK SEAT.
PREPARED ENOUGH FOR YA?
POLICE ISSUE. REDDNER RAVAGER .50 TACTICAL ASSAULT SPECIAL.
YOU LIKE IT?
IT'S VERY NICE.
WHERE ARE WE GOING?
THE CHATEAU.
YOU KNOW WHERE IT IS.

SO HOW COME YOU QUIT BEING A DETECTIVE, MCBLACK?
YOU SEEM TO BE PRETTY GOOD AT IT.
I JUST KIND OF LOST INTEREST.
YOU GOT BORED?
REALIZED THAT THE ONLY PART OF THE JOB I REALLY ENJOYED WAS THE BIT WHERE I GOT TO SHOOT PEOPLE OR BLOW SHIT UP.
I DECIDED TO CONCENTRATE ON THAT.
MUCH BETTER MONEY IN MAYHEM?
IT'S NOT ABOUT MONEY, IT'S ABOUT WORK/LIFE BALANCE. JOB SATISFACTION.
YOU DON'T HAVE A LIFE, MCBLACK.
I'M NOT EVEN SURE YOU COUNT AS BEING ALIVE.
FIGURE OF SPEECH.
AH, HERE WE ARE.

OH, GOOD. EVERYONE'S HERE ALREADY.
WHAT IS THIS, A TEA PARTY?
LADIES' AUXILIARY-- BUT IT'S GONNA BE A REAL SHORT ONE.
NICE BOOTS, BY THE WAY.
WELL, THEY'RE ACTUALLY YOURS.
HI, EVERYONE.
I THINK MOST OF YOU KNOW EACH OTHER ALREADY.

LADIES AND GENTLEMEN, I HAVE GATHERED YOU HERE TODAY--
HI.
HI.
LADIES AND GENTLEMEN--
YOU ARE FUCKINK ZIS SCHWEIN, NOW? ZIS PIG?
WHAT IF I AM?
YOU'RE FUCKING THE MILKMAN.
AH DON'T CARE WHO IS FUCKING WHO-- AH WANT MAH DRUGS OR I WANT MY MONEY BACK.
I WANT ME GUNS, BEJAYSUS 'N' BEGORRA.
YOU'RE NOT GETTING ANY GUNS UNTIL I GET PAID IN FULL.
GUNS? DRUGS? FORGET ALL THAT SHIT--
WHERE'S THE DELUCCI BAMBINO?

LADIES AND GENTLEMEN, I HAV[E] GATHERED YOU AL[L] HERE TODAY--
AHEM.
ENOUGH THEATRICS. JUST TELL US WHERE OBERG IS SO WE CAN GET ON WITH IT.
BOOGEDY BOOGAH, BEGORRA!
YEAH!
JA!
GOD-DAMN RIGHT!
AYE!

MY GUESS IS, HE SPLIT TOWN WEEKS AGO.
I DON'T KNOW WHERE HE IS.
YOU SAID WE WERE COMING HERE TO FINISH THIS!
WE ARE.
LADIES AND GENTLEMEN, I HAVE GATHERED YOU HERE TODAY BECAUSE I'VE HAD ENOUGH OF THIS WHOLE THING AND I WANT TO PUT AN END TO IT.
I HAVE GATHERED YOU ALL HERE TODAY IN ORDER TO MORE CONVENIENTLY KILL YOU ALL.
THANK YOU FOR YOUR PARTICIPATION.
YOU'VE BEEN WONDERFUL.

THE FAT COP FIRST,
BECAUSE I HATE HIM.

THE REST ARE
STILL IN SLOW MO.

JAYNA,
TAKE CARE OF
THESE IDIOTS.

DON'T LIKE THE SHAMAN'S
LEPRECHAUN HAT, SO HE
GOES NEXT.

AND THEN IT'S MY TURN.
OUCH! RIGHT IN THE BLOOD BAG.
I'M DOWN FOR THE COUNT--
BUT THE CROWD IS KIND ENOUGH TO CARRY ON WITHOUT ME.

NOW THIS WHAT YOU PAID YOUR DOLLAR FOR--AM I RIGHT?

KUNG FU FIGHTING. BEHEADINGS AND GUNSMOKE.
FEEL FREE TO SING ALONG.

I'M A POET, AND DON'T I KNOW IT.

JAYNA TRIES TO PUT ME DOWN AGAIN.
THIS TIME I SHOOT BACK. 
WE BOTH GET SOME NEW HOLES IN US.
LUCKY FOR ME, I WAS HOLLOW TO BEGIN WITH.

THE BOARDOGS TAKE THE HIGH GROUND. SMART MOVE.

BUT ME? I ALWAYS PREFERRED TO STAY LOW.

HEY, ZIGGY!

ZAG.
I'M SO CLEVER.

I KILL ME.
UH, HI THERE.

GROUP HUG?
SOMETIMES I'M JUST TOO CUDDLY FOR MY OWN GOOD.

NO?

WELL, HOW 'BOUT A HAND GRENADE, THEN?
PLINK!
BOOM.

I'M REALLY IMPRESSED BY THIS GUY.

YOU JUST DON'T SEE THIS KIND OF MACHETE WORK ANYMORE.

PERSONALLY? I BLAME VIDEO GAMES.

DEATH
BE YOURS,
MON.

UH, WHAT
HE SAID.

LIKE, WHOA, DUDE.
I'M PRETTY SURE THE LAST TIME WE MET, I PUT A BULLET IN YOUR HEAD.
YOU DESTROYED MY THIRD EYE, MAN.
I SAW BEYOND THE VEIL.
THAT BULLET SHOWED ME... WONDERS...
HUH. REALLY?
WELL, LET'S SEE WHAT A WHOLE CLIP DOES FOR YOU.

I'VE BEEN BEYOND THE VEIL, TOO.
I MEAN, COME ON. I KNOW I'M WEIRD, BUT YOU DON'T THINK I WAS BORN THIS WAY, DO YOU?

I'VE PASSED THROUGH THE PEARLY GATES AND THE DEVIL'S ARSEHOLE.
I'VE SEEN THE BIG ROCK CANDY MOUNTAINS, THE HALLS OF VALHALLA, THE END OF THE RAINBOW.

I'VE MET ANGELS AND ELVES; KARMA POLICE AND BLUE MEANIES. GREY UFO-GUYS AND LITTLE GREEN MARTIANS.

FAR AS I'M CONCERNED, THE ONLY GOOD PART OF THE SWEET HEREAFTER IS THAT YOU NEVER RUN OUT OF AMMUNITION.

YOU CAN COME OUT, NOW.
EVERY-BODY ELSE IS DEAD.

WOW, IT'S REALLY KIND OF... FUNKY... IN HERE.
THAT'S JUST MY COLOGNE. 'ABATTOIR FRESH'.
SO, IT'S TRUE? MY EX-HUSBAND REALLY LEFT TOWN?

RECKON SO.

I HIRED YOU TO FIND HIM.
NO, YOU DIDN'T.

YOU HIRED ME BECAUSE YOU KNEW I'D WIND UP KILLING EVERYONE THAT EVER DID BUSINESS WITH HIM.

I CHECKED THE PUBLIC RECORDS-- YOU WEREN'T MARRIED TO HIM FOR LONG.
OBERG WAS UP TO HIS EYEBALLS IN BAD DEALS: THE BOARDOGS, THE E.I.R.A, THE TRIADS...
HE THOUGHT YOUR MONEY WOULD SOLVE HIS PROBLEMS.
BUT THAT WASN'T TRUE, WAS IT?
YOU AND LOVER-BOY HERE HAVE YOUR OWN DEBTS, AND OBERG ASSUMED THEM WHEN HE TOOK ON YOUR TITLES.
BUT OBERG WAS SMARTER THAN YOU FIGURED.
ONCE HE WORKED IT OUT HE WAS GONE LIKE THE WIND, AND YOU TWO WERE IN TWICE THE MESS YOU STARTED WITH.
AND SO YOU BROUGHT ME IN.
HE'S GOT US THERE, HON.
HEY, I GOTTA ASK:
WHAT'S THE DEAL WITH THAT SOCCER TEAM?
UH, I THOUGHT THAT WAS YOU? I DIDN'T INVITE THEM.
NOPE. WASN'T ME.
AT THIS POINT, WHO CARES?
IT'S ALL OVER NOW.

I JUST STAND THERE AND TAKE IT.
THESE CLOTHES ARE ALREADY RUINED.

EVENTUALLY, THEY RUN OUT OF AMMUNITION.
WELL, I THINK THAT'S ENOUGH OF THAT, 'EY? ANY LAST WORDS? PITHY ONE-LINERS? PERHAPS BIT OF POETRY?
NOPE?

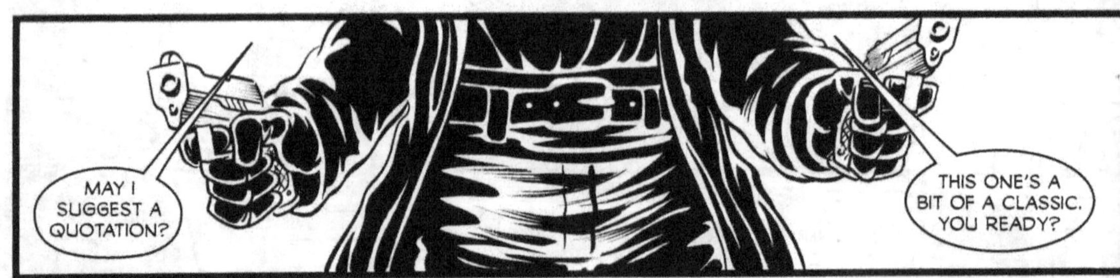

MAY I SUGGEST A QUOTATION?
THIS ONE'S A BIT OF A CLASSIC. YOU READY?

'BYE BYE, BLACKIE.'

IT'S ONE OF MY FAVOURITES.

OH, COME ON.
YOU KNEW IT WASN'T GOING TO BE A FAIR FIGHT.
YOU ALWAYS KNEW THAT I WAS GONNA WIN.
'CAUSE I'M THE GOOD GUY, RIGHT?
I'M THE HERO.
'CAUSE I'M THE NARRATOR OF THE STORY.
THANKS FOR YOUR PARTICIPATION.

YOU'VE BEEN WONDERFUL.
3: ON THE RICOCHET

THE BALLAD OF McBLACK

They found McBlack up to his ankles in blood,
Cordite burns on his forehead a wreath;
Red feet and black hands, eyes cold and bright,
And a smile that showed all of his teeth.

Smiling, McBlack confessed all to the judge;
He laughed, as they cut off his feet,
"Pound on the drums and strum your guitars,
In my boots I can yet dance the beat."

McBlack gave the jury a two-finger salute,
He sang while they sawed off his wrists:
"I'll worry no more about fingerprints, then,
"And my gloves have a much firmer grip."

"Bit more elbow grease, girls," quoth he, the condemned,
As they twisted his legs off his hips,
"Button my fly if you're finished down there,
And remember to wipe off your lips."

McBlack hummed a jig as they pulled out his arms;
He sang in a voice sweet and rough:
"Ladies, from now on its Xes, not Os,
"And I guess I'll just roll down my cuffs."

McBlack wasn't so pleased when they shaved off his hair,
But he was damned if he'd give them a rise:
"It was bleached by the sun and it hung from my head
"But my hat keeps the glare from my eyes."

McBlack was impressed when they struck off his head,
for the axeman took only three strokes;
"I'll turn up my collar," spake his wicker-bound head,
"I always felt that necktie was a yoke."

McBlack didn't blink when they burned out his eyes,
and threaded a hook through his sockets,
"My baby blues always looked better in black,
"But good shades are so hard on my pockets."

Birds ate McBlack's face while he swung from the chain;
His quartz jaws shone far whiter than bone.
"I'm embarrassed," said he, through his black razor teeth,
"Hanging 'round here without any clothes."

JASON FRANKS

can write just about anything, so long as there's a double-digit bodycount and the baddies win.

Franks is the author of the occult rock'n'roll novel, BLOODY WATERS, the LEFT HAND PATH series, and THE SIXMITHS graphic novels. His work has been shortlisted for Aurealis and Ledger awards.

Franks' second novel, FAERIE APOCALYPSE, will be out in 2017 from IFWG Australia.

http://www.jasonfranks.com

DAVE GUTIERREZ

is a professional tattoo artist, architect, penciller, inker, colorist, and punk rock guitarist.

Gutierrez is best known for inking the works of comic book legend Gene Colan, and for illustrating graphic novel BILLBOARDS (written by Clifford Meth).

In 2008, VEI Press published ABSTRACT REALITY; a full colour, hardcover volume containing more than 50 works by Gutierrez: trippy pen and ink drawings, detailed pencil illustrations, serene watercolors, masterful inks over Gene Colan's pencils, and sequential art storytelling.

http://abstractreality.net

OUT NOW:
SMILING
DAMNED
FRANKS | WATTS | HALYDAY | FAYE | QUEST | JONES
COLOUR ME!
FEATURING A BRAND
NEW STORY STARRIN
WHITEFACE McBLACK!